Ocean Hide and Seek

by Jennifer Evans Kramer
illustrated by Gary R. Phillips

The living sea is very wide—
very wide, very wide.
So many places there to hide,
where sand and restless sea collide.

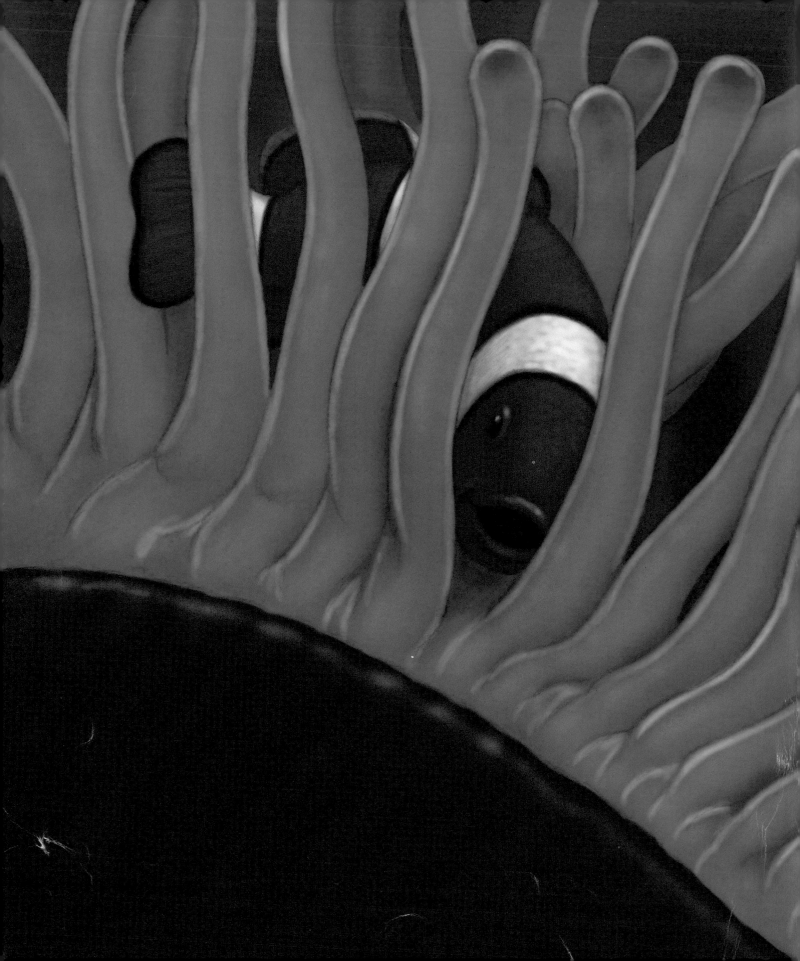

Clownfish colors, orange and white—
orange and white, orange and white.
Seeking shelter, taking flight,
clownfish hiding in plain sight.

Through the darkness, eyes that see—
eyes that see, eyes that see.
A catshark swimming, wild and free,
hunting prey beneath the sea.

Bands of color, dark and light—
dark and light, dark and light.
A whale shark swimming into sight,
fades like shadows in the night.

Floating there, before our eyes—
before our eyes, before our eyes.
A seaweed curtain bares its prize,
a tiny dragon in disguise.

From up above or down below—
down below, down below.
The light conceals what colors show,
and makes the shark a sneaky foe.

Brighten, lighten, give and take—
give and take, give and take.
A bristlemouth knows what's at stake,
and leaves no outlines in its wake.

Shifting, sifting, blue to gray—
blue to gray, blue to gray.
A school of tangs now swims away,
cloaked in colors of the day.

In beds of kelp, beneath each swell—
beneath each swell, beneath each swell.
Tiny crabs can safely dwell,
bits of weed upon each shell.

Clever arms that dip and sway—
dip and sway, dip and sway.
Like deadly sea snakes seeking prey,
predators soon swim away.

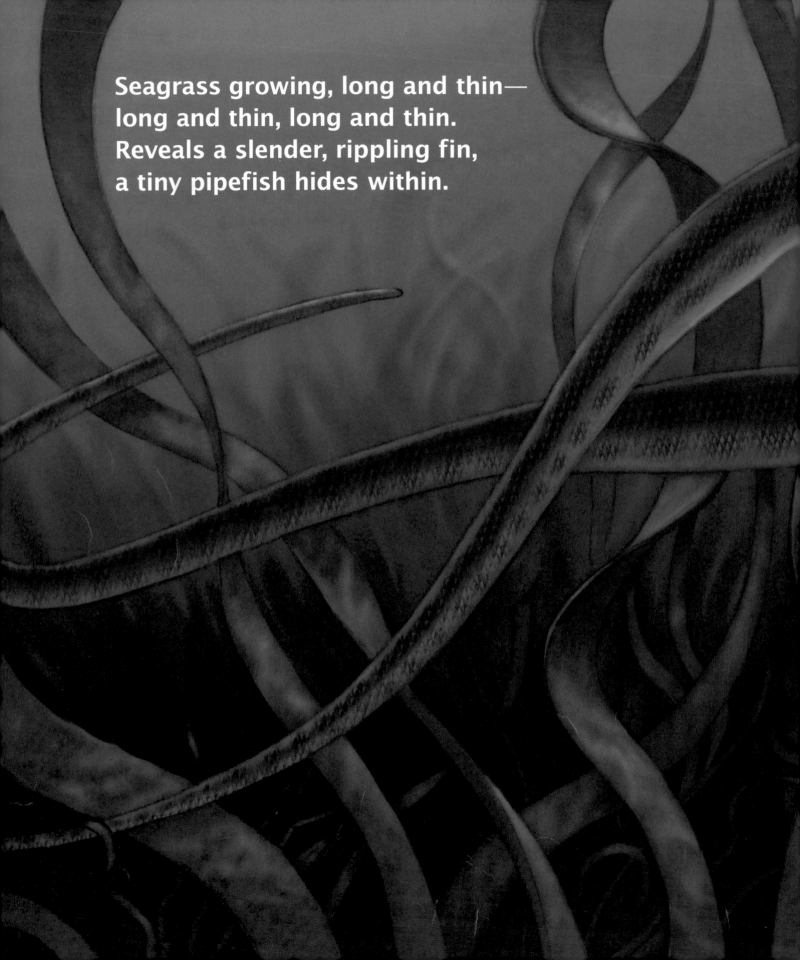

Seagrass growing, long and thin—
long and thin, long and thin.
Reveals a slender, rippling fin,
a tiny pipefish hides within.

Though dark of night is falling soon—
falling soon, falling soon.
Along the reef, a brilliant moon
reveals a queen in her cocoon.

The living sea is very old—
very old, very old.
So many stories still untold,
so many wonders to behold.

For Creative Minds

Animal Hide and Seek

Do you like to play hide and seek? For animals, this game is a matter of life or death. Prey must hide or risk becoming another animal's next meal. Sometimes a predator hides and waits for its meal to come swimming by! Either way, camouflage helps these animals survive.

Look for the picture of the animal listed in bold to see the camouflage description.

Hiding in Plain Sight

When an animal matches the color of its environment, it is called *cryptic camouflage*. Many fishes and sharks have colors that blend into the water. But what about spots and stripes? On land, a tiger's stripes help it blend in with the tall grass and break up the tiger's outline. This makes it hard to see how big it is. This is known as *disruptive coloration*. Many ocean animals have spots or stripes, from fish (including **clownfish**) to eels, rays, and even **catsharks**. If you are as big as a **whale shark**, it is good to have both!

Pretending to be Something Else

If it looks like a sea snake and slides like a sea snake, it must be a sea snake—right? Not always. *Mimicry* is when one animal copies how another animal looks. When attacked by grouper, a **mimic octopus** can look like the deadly sea snake. The grouper avoid it at all costs. Wouldn't you?

Transparency

Being as clear as glass (like a **jellyfish**) is another important way to avoid being seen.

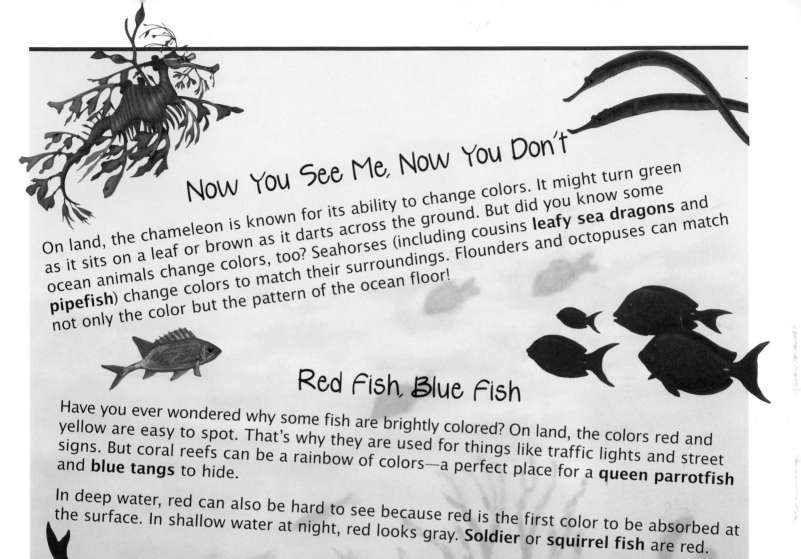

Now You See Me, Now You Don't

On land, the chameleon is known for its ability to change colors. It might turn green as it sits on a leaf or brown as it darts across the ground. But did you know some ocean animals change colors, too? Seahorses (including cousins **leafy sea dragons** and **pipefish**) change colors to match their surroundings. Flounders and octopuses can match not only the color but the pattern of the ocean floor!

Red Fish, Blue Fish

Have you ever wondered why some fish are brightly colored? On land, the colors red and yellow are easy to spot. That's why they are used for things like traffic lights and street signs. But coral reefs can be a rainbow of colors—a perfect place for a **queen parrotfish** and **blue tangs** to hide.

In deep water, red can also be hard to see because red is the first color to be absorbed at the surface. In shallow water at night, red looks gray. **Soldier** or **squirrel fish** are red.

Light from Inside

Counter illumination is when an animal lights up its own body from the inside, so the outline of its dark body can't be seen. Squid and some types of fish, like the deep-sea **bristlemouth**, can seem almost invisible to other animals hunting in the waters below.

Bubbles

Some **parrotfish** make a clear, mucus "sleeping bag" cocoon at night. The mucus covers their scent, making it more difficult for predators to find them.

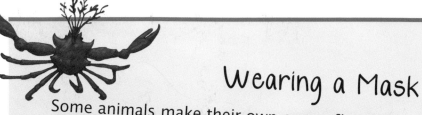

Wearing a Mask

Some animals make their own camouflage. *Masking* is when an animal uses something in its environment to hide itself. Some **crabs** hide by sticking bits of kelp to their shells. Talk about playing with your food!

Shape Up!

For some animals, hiding is not just about color—it's about shape too. The **leafy sea dragon** has leaf-like flaps of skin and floats among sea plants. Stonefish, as you might guess, look like stones. **Pipefish** look like the blades of grass in which they live.

Darkness and Light

Sharks, whales, and rays have dark backs and light bellies. This is known as *counter shading*. To animals swimming above them, the dark color blends in with the dark water below. To animals swimming below them, the light color blends in with the sunlit water above.

Watch Out!

Sometimes bright colors warn of danger. Orange and white **clownfish** can often be found among the tentacles of the sea anemone. The sea anemone looks like a harmless plant but is really an animal with a poisonous sting. The clownfish makes special mucus to protect itself from the sting. Other sea creatures are not so lucky! The bright orange of the clownfish may warn other animals to stay away from the anemone's poison!

Animal Classification

Fish are not the only type of animals that live in the ocean. Just as there are many different classes of animals that live on land, there are many classes of animals that live in the ocean.

Marine reptiles (sea turtles and sea snakes) and **mammals** (dolphins and whales) come to the surface to breathe the air they need. Other marine animals can get their oxygen from the water.

Fish are divided into *two major groups*: **fish with bones** and **fish with cartilage** (like our ears) instead of bones. Sharks and rays are examples of fishes with cartilage. Angelfish and parrotfish are examples of fishes with bones.

Invertebrates are animals without a backbone. More than 90% of all animals on earth are invertebrates. This includes **mollusks** (whelks, conchs, octopuses, clams, oysters), worms, and **arthropods** (insects, crustaceans, spiders), among others.

cartilage fish	bony fish	mollusk	arthropod

Food for Thought

What are some of the things you do when you hide during a game of hide and seek? You might hide in or behind something—animals do, too.

Imagine if you could change your skin color to blend into your surroundings. In fact, if you look at an Army camouflage outfit, that's what soldiers do with their clothes!

To what color would you change your skin to hide in or around . . .

water   sand   snow   mud

grass   rocks   leaves   trees

The author is donating a portion of her royalties to the National Marine Sanctuary Foundation. "Each footprint may be small, but together they create a trail for others to follow. Our seas are home to some of the earth's most valuable treasures, an abundance of plant and animal life that we are just beginning to learn about and understand. Once lost, these treasures may disappear forever. Education is the first step to preserving and protecting this ecosystem, and providing future generations with a priceless legacy."—JEK

To my dad, Randall Evans, who taught me to read; to my husband, Andrew, who taught me to believe; to my children, Mitchell, Patrick, Jessica & Jeffrey, who taught me to dream; and to my son's teacher, Mrs. Debbie Kelley, who inspired both me and my son to learn about one of earth's most precious resources, its oceans.—JEK

To Mom and Dad who always allowed me to swim into the depths.—GRP

Thanks to Nancee Hunter, Oregon Sea Grant Director of Education at Hatfield Marine Science Center; Dr. Michael Vecchione of the NMFS National Systematics Laboratory at the Smithsonian National Museum of Natural History; and Allison Byrd, Education Coordinator for the Consortium for Ocean Leadership for verifying the accuracy of the information in this book.

Publisher's Cataloging-In-Publication Data

Kramer, Jennifer E.

Ocean hide and seek / by Jennifer Evans Kramer ;
illustrated by Gary R. Phillips.

p. : col. ill. ; cm.

Summary: The ocean is an old, old place, and the exotic animals in the depths have learned to adapt to their surroundings to survive. Can you find the creatures hidden on every page? Includes "For Creative Minds" educational section.

Interest age level: 004-008.
Interest grade level: P-3.
ISBN: 978-1-934359-91-4 (hardcover)
ISBN: 978-1-607180-36-4 (pbk.)
ISBN: 978-1-607180-56-2 (eBook)
ISBN: 978-1-607180-46-3 (Spanish eBook)

1. Marine animals--Juvenile literature. 2. Picture puzzles--Juvenile literature. 3. Camouflage (Biology)--Juvenile literature. 4. Marine animals. 5. Picture puzzles. 6. Stories in rhyme. I. Phillips, Gary R. II. Title.

QL122.2 .K73 2009
591.77   2008936037

Printed in China

Sylvan Dell Publishing
976 Houston Northcutt Blvd., Suite 3
Mt. Pleasant, SC 29464